Eve   hat...

Do   ce!

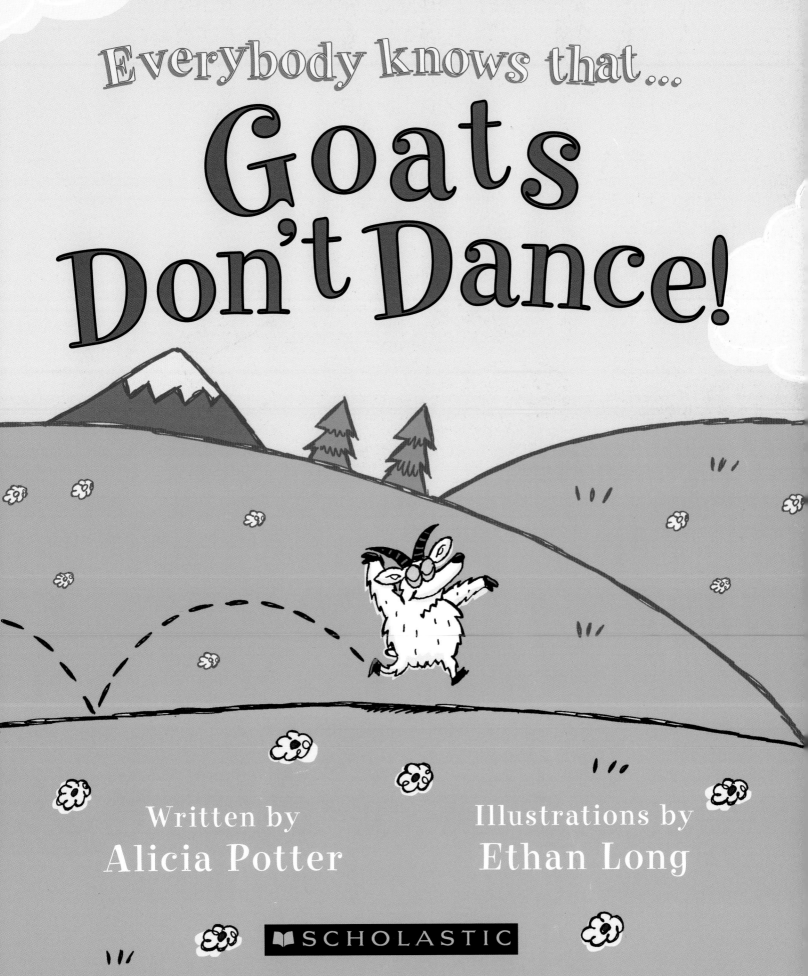

Everybody knows that...

Goats Don't Dance!

Written by
Alicia Potter

Illustrations by
Ethan Long

SCHOLASTIC

Not many goats
danced the fandango . . .

but George did.

He danced beneath the fir trees.

He danced among the heather.

He danced atop his favourite rock.

He loved the sound of his hooves.

CLIP-CLIP-CLIPPETY-CLOP!

The other goats snickered.
They snorted.
They laughed their tails off.

Their snickers hurt George's ears.

Their snorts made his hooves feel heavy.

Like they'd lost their clip.

And their clop.

"I don't belong in this herd," he said.

"I need to find some dancing goats."

George imagined all the clipping.

He imagined all the clopping.

He imagined his pick of partners.

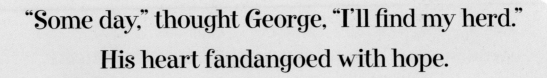

"Some day," thought George, "I'll find my herd."
His heart fandangoed with hope.

So one morning, when the sun
was so bright, and the fields so buttercuppy,
George couldn't stop his hooves.
He danced over the stile . . .

across the pasture . . .

and past the stream, until he couldn't hear
a single snicker or snort or laugh.

In a meadow,
he came upon a sheep named Liesl.
"Excuse me," said George.
"But do you know any goats who
dance the fandango?"
"The fan-whato?" asked Liesl.

"The fandango," said George.

He showed her a few steps.

CLIP-CLIP-CLIPPETY-CLOP!

"Nope," said Liesl. "But I yodel.

YODEL-LAY-HEEEEEEEEEEEE-EWE!
YODELY-YODELY-HOO-HOO!"

"It's no fandango," she said, "but I like it.
The head ewe said it turned
her stomachs – all four of them – and so
I left the flock."

"Come with me," George said.
"I'd like the company while I find a new herd."
"I'd be happy to!" said Liesl.

George and Liesl shambled down ravines . . .
and gambolled up hills.

On the next alp,
they came upon a dog named
Max, dozing in the shade.
"Excuse me," said George.
"But do you know any goats
who dance the fandango?"
"Fan-who?" asked Max.

"The fandango." George showed him
a few steps.

CLIP-CLIP-CLIPPETY-CLOP!

"No," said Max.
"But let me show *you* something."

He returned with a strange musical instrument.

"I play the glockenspiel," said Max.

PING-PING-A-LING-DING!

"It's no fandango," said Max, "but it suits me.

Unfortunately, my shepherd said it distracts the flock."

"Come with us," George said.

"We need some help finding my herd."

"At your service," said Max.

George, Liesl, and Max
loped through pastures.

They climbed
and climbed.
And they practised.

CLIP-CLIP-CLIPPETY-CLOP!
YODEL-LAY-HEEEEEEEEEEEE-EWE!
PING-PING-A-LING-DING!

They encountered many goats.
But not one danced the hokey-cokey,
never mind the fandango.

One day, George wandered off,
alone and sad,
to the other side of a hill.

"There must be something we can do," said Max.
"Yes," said Liesl. "But what?"

Liesl and Max thought about
all the goats they'd ever met.
They thought about the most
musical beasts they knew.

"There's you," said Max.
"And you," replied Liesl.
"But we've never
danced the fandango."

George sighed. "Will I *ever* find my herd?
Am I destined to dance alone?"
His hooves felt heavy.
Like they'd lost their clip. And their clop.

But soon George began to miss more
than a dancing partner. He missed Liesl and Max.

Just then, a sound wafted to George's ears.
It was the sound of hooves. Dancing hooves.
"Could it be?" whispered George.

George galloped up . . . up . . . up the hill.
At the top he found . . .

... Liesl and Max dancing the fandango!

"How did you learn to dance like that?" asked George.

"We watched you so often . . ." panted Max.

" . . . We taught ourselves," finished Liesl.

George, Liesl, and Max fandangoed
like there was no tomorrow.

They **CLIP-CLIP-CLIPPETY-CLOPPED!**

They **YODEL-LAY-HEEEEEEEEEEE-EWED!**

They even took turns **PING-PING-A-LINGING**

on Max's glockenspiel.

The trio made quite a noise on the buttercuppy hills.

George sighed.
"Finally, I've found my herd!" he said.
His heart fandangoed with joy.

First published in 2009 by Scholastic Inc
This edition first published in 2010 by Scholastic Children's Books
Euston House, 24 Eversholt Street
London NW1 1DB
a division of Scholastic Ltd
www.scholastic.co.uk

London · New York · Toronto · Sydney · Auckland
Mexico City · New Delhi · Hong Kong

Text copyright © 2009 Alicia Potter
Illustrations copyright © 2009 Ethan Long

ISBN 978 1407 11498 9

The moral rights of Alicia Potter and Ethan Long have been asserted.

Papers used by Scholastic Children's Books are made from wood grown in sustainable forests.

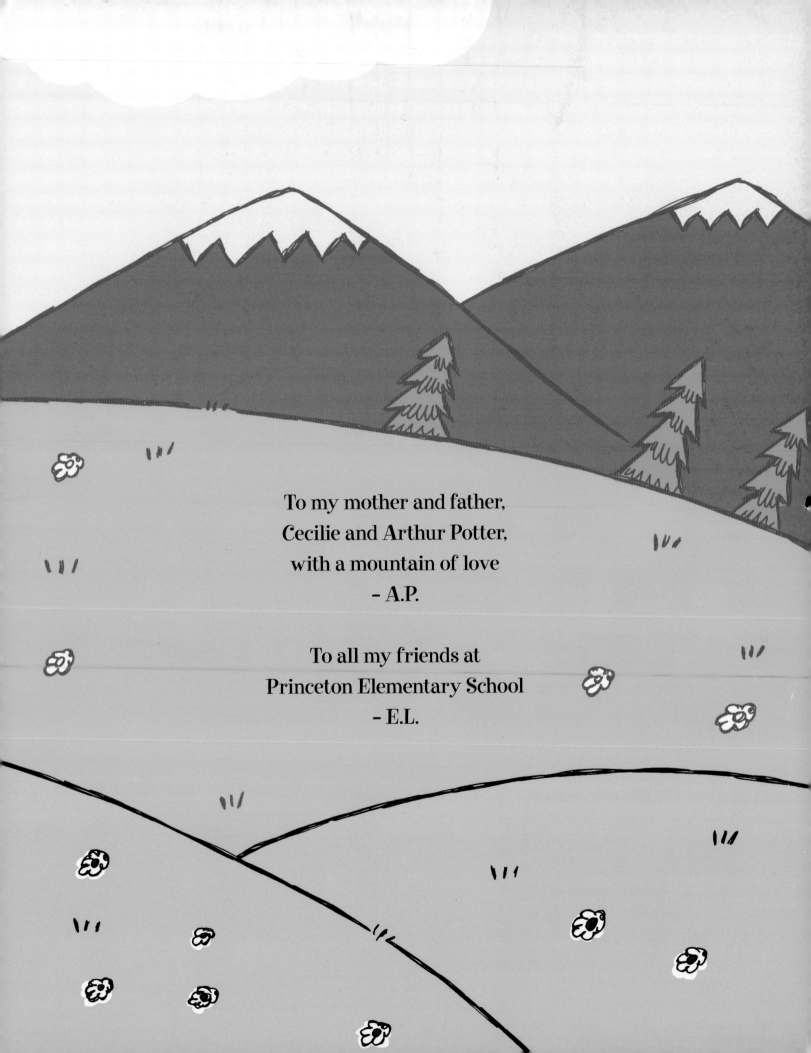

To my mother and father,
Cecilie and Arthur Potter,
with a mountain of love
– A.P.

To all my friends at
Princeton Elementary School
– E.L.